A TROUBADOURS
SHORT STORY

Nici's Christmas Tale

1157: AQUITAINE

JEAN GILL

Copyright © Jean Gill 2018
The 13th Sign
ISBN 979-10-96459-13-1

All rights reserved. No part of this publication may be reproduced, stored in a retrieval system, or transmitted in any form without prior permission from the publisher

Cover design – Jessica Bell.
Artwork © Jean Gill
(dogs and French landscapes in snow),
LadyMary (silver border)

*For Sherlock and Watson,
my second chance dogs*

CHAPTER ONE

Snow blasted into the sheepfold through every gap in the wooden door, stone walls and roof tiles, sprinkling white on the pens. Beasts huddled for woolly warmth, fleeces curling where the damp flurries had reached them. Such an angry wind could find a way through the tiniest crack in the most solid building so it was no reflection on the lords of Breyault that their sheep were cold this night.

The humans could be forgiven for distraction. Not only was it Christmas Eve but it was the long night of a woman's natural pain. The wind howled on her behalf and the household held its breath.

In the sheepfold, amid their bleating companions, three mountain dogs paced, unsettled by threats against which they could do nothing but wait. The blizzard would pass. One of them had lived through worse and said so in his deep voice.

'We need fear neither wolf nor bear when the white wind wreaks its worst,' Nici growled, intending to reassure his pack. In truth, wolf or bear would have been easier for him than this wait, jumping at every noise.

'You're frightening the sheep, Nici.' It was the bitch, Peldolce, who replied, from the hay-strewn corner of a pen where a pile of puppies snuggled in her warmth. Their cream fur blended into the yellowed fleeces around them so the untrained eye would not notice the difference, until the protector showed his teeth. That mistake had been the last one made by many a wolf or bear on a dark mountain night. Bears were allowed to run away, harried by the dogs, but wolves, they killed.

'Stupid creatures!' was the reply of the dog known as Nici, his name also meaning 'Stupid' in the language of Aquitaine where they lived. There had been a time when *he* was thought to be the stupid animal. Nobody pointed this out to him.

'Not in front of the puppies, Nici,' warned his mate, in a voice closer to purr than growl. 'This will be their job one day, if we raise them as we should.'

Nici stopped pacing, looked at the sleeping pile of fur. 'Maybe,' he conceded, his tone softening.

The other pair of dogs had automatically formed a triangle with Nici when he stood still, facing outwards, so they covered any danger that might come. They had covered for each other so many summer nights on the open hills that the habit stayed over winter, although the barn was locked and should be safe.

As they stood guard, the great wooden door shook. A shadow showed through the crack. A human shadow, looming wrongly tall and flickering against horizontal gusts of snow.

'Nici,' growled the dog nearest the door, low and urgent.

'I see him.'

A puppy squealed its waking hunger and was shushed.

Slowly, the key turned in the lock and then the door blew open, carrying the stranger into the fold, with enough snow to form a ridge that tripped him up. He landed, clutching a huge iron key and laughing softly, as if three sets of bared teeth were a game he'd played before. Four sets, as the bitch was on her feet, shaking off the puppies, ready to defend them to the death.

But it *was* a game he'd played before.

'Musca! You shouldn't be here!' Nici's voice was gruff but his nudge to help the little boy to his feet was as gentle as it was firm. More giggles were the only result but when the dogs used their strength to battle the door closed again, Musca understood what they wanted and turned the key in the lock once more.

By now, the puppies were awake, and Musca dived under the wooden rail and into the straw to join them in their pen. They were still small enough, and he old enough, to pick up each wriggling bundle, tickle a tummy and return it to its siblings for more energetic games.

'I couldn't sleep,' he informed the animals around him, as if they understood every word. 'Mama and Papa said that Raoulf would look after me and I must not disturb anybody or mind any noises I might hear, that all would be well tomorrow as it is Christmas Day. But Raoulf got called away by the men because Papa is not to be disturbed and he thought I was asleep and I wasn't but I was frightened by the wind so I'm here. If I was seven I wouldn't be frightened because then I'd be a man and have my own proper longbow. But I'm still six and I wish you could tell me what's happening.' Musca put his arms round Nici's neck, and lay half across his back as he'd done since he first learned to toddle.

Normally, Nici would have escorted Musca back to bed. It was nearly midnight and a small boy, *his* small boy, should not be in the sheepfold. But tonight was not normal and this was the safest place for Musca until the travail in the chateau was over, for good or ill, and someone came looking for him.

Nici bit back a howl of frustration. He should be with his mistress. Not banished like the boy beside him, her son. He'd end up pacing and that would send the sheep into a frenzy.

A sleepy puppy waddled over to Nici. 'Papa, tell us a story.'

Before he could growl no, Nici had two puppies swinging from his chin by their teeth while their siblings joined a chorus of 'Story, story, story!'

Nici gently swatted the two climbers onto the straw and then lay down, to allow his offspring gentler contact. 'No teeth,' he reminded them, as he leaned against the wooden manger that split the barn in two lengthways. Goodness only knew how Peldolce put up with them suckling. Sometimes she didn't.

'Tell the bit where blood dripped in the dark forest,' prompted Reymarca, a pup with a beige crown of fur on his creamy forehead. 'Ouch!' He reacted to his brother's nip with a quick lunge.

'Boys!' warned Nici.

'Tell about snuggling in the ditch.'

'About the nasty shepherd.'

'About the moment you knew for sure,' demanded one of the more romantic pups.

'Good stories begin at the beginning.' Nici was firm.

'And this is the best of stories,' woofed Peldolce, as she lay beside her mate and warmed her share of puppies.

Musca burrowed in among the creamy fur, avoiding claws and sharp little teeth, made a nest for himself and shut his eyes. Yaps, barks, whines, growls and bleats reverberated, keeping out the storm fears. The straw-sweet smell of puppies mixed with damp wool and reminded him of the strengthening posset his mother gave him when he had winter sneezes.

His insides clenched shut. He wasn't allowed to go to his mother tonight and nobody would know if he sneaked childhood comfort. He grasped Nici's fur with one hand, coarse and yet more comforting than the puppies' silk. He allowed the other hand to drift to his mouth and, sucking his thumb, eyes shut, he listened to the rumbling voice of his big protector, the dog who had been his friend since before memory.

CHAPTER TWO

'I was born in a sheepfold just like this,' Nici began.

'When the wind howled like a monster,' a puppy added helpfully, 'and the snow piled drifts as big as a chateau's tallness–'

'Too soon for lambing.'

'And too late to feed up the ewes,' contributed two squeaky voices.

'Probably,' agreed Nici while the others shushed the would-be storytellers.

'I was born in the land of heath and sheep, of caves and blue cheese, somewhere in the fief of Carcassonne. And I was born to be a pastou, a dog who guarded sheep. I knew the tickle of straw in my nose and the smooth tongues of my barn-mates, brothers, sisters, goats and sheep.

I also knew my mother's rough tongue but I never knew my father's. His heart burst before I was born, and now he was part of the mountain and the river, my mother told me as she washed my ears.'

The wind had found a zig-zag chink in the stone and played an eerie whistle through the crack. Sheep chomped on straws, sucking them out of the manger and vying for the middle, whether because the fodder was sweeter there or because where one went, all followed. However long he spent with sheep, Nici could never understand their ways. But he had been born among them and their smell was part of his story.

'I don't believe you were ever young like us.' One rebel sat up and looked his father in the chin.

'More like you than you know.' Nici cuffed his small likeness and continued. 'Our shepherd, Jehan-Pastor gave us food and water out of the sheep's reach so they couldn't steal our bread and foul our drink.' He glanced at Peldolce, mindful of her censorship regarding the less desirable qualities of sheep. However, if the puppies were to become good pastous, they had to know the truth about their charges.

Fixing Peldolce in an unblinking gaze, Nici added, 'And it was just as well we could play in our own pen until we learned our manners.' Here he glared at his sons. 'I know of one puppy who left his pen and was so rude that the ram attacked him! Even when his bruises healed, that puppy was so frightened he could never do his job.' Nine little furry bodies shrank closer to the sheltering flanks of the adult dogs, well away from ovine hooves and horns.

'When we were old enough, our mother presented us to the ram. When he sniffed us, we were accepted. But the ram is not the leader of the sheep-pack. Jehan-Pastor knew his flock and he gave extra salt to some ewes that he chose carefully.

One of these he selected as the leader. He gave her bread to tame her and he put a calf-bell round her neck. She was always first out of the fold on a fine day but she'd hang back if she knew the storm was coming. Jehan-Pastor would watch her at night. If she shook her fleece and rang her bell, the next day would be cold. He had lots of tricks like that to tell the weather. Humans have no sense of smell so they can't tell what the wind is bringing unless they observe wiser creatures.

When we were introduced to the bellwether she lowered her horns and stamped her feet, so we retreated to our pen. Mother tried again the next day and the day after that. Each time, the bell-wether was less intimidating until the day when, finally, she condescended to sniff us. She let me lick her face and the whole flock saw we were their pastous.

From that day, we learned the ways of Jehan-Pastor and his flock. On cold winter mornings when he rose late, he shared his soup with us. On early summer mornings, he fed us bread from his wicker panier, out in the pastures while the sheep grazed. He judged the season for every task, including my initiation to adulthood.

'It is your time,' he told me and he cut the ear of a sheep till beads of blood made bite demands to my nose. I took the ear between my teeth. 'Good dog,' Jehan-Pastor told me. I did not bite down.

'Good dog,' Jehan-Pastor told me. 'Bring the sheep here. Bring him here.' I'd seen my mother take a sheep by its ear to steer it to safety so I did too, enjoying the blood-taste in my mouth.

Jehan-Pastor was so excited he gave me salt as well as praise. 'From now on, you will never touch a sheep except by the ear,' he told me. And so I didn't. If the sheep was alive.

Dead ewes were a different matter and I soon learned how to tell when a sheep became mutton and I was allowed to eat her. 'Three days,' Jehan-Pastor said but I knew by the smell.

At first, my litter-mates learned with me but different shepherds visited and, one at a time, the others went to pastures new. When I was the only one left with Mother, Jehan-Pastor took the rope out of his panier and tied me to a tree, for a short time. Each day he tied me longer, 'to get me used to it.' I hated the constraint but I'd seen Mother tied this way sometimes and she accepted it. So I did too.

Sometimes, Jehan-Pastor made me walk beside him on the rope, in a big circle round the flock and when I barked, he praised me. He made me lie down and he crossed my front paws. I uncrossed them. He crossed them again. I uncrossed them. He sighed and crossed them a third time.

'Don't be a bad dog,' he growled at me. I left my paws crossed and this pleased him.

'Now you know how to lie still and do guard duty,' he told me.

Each season had its rhythm and its dangers. In March, Jehan-Patou spent two days fasting and praying before he cropped the little tails and testicles of the January lambs.

'Three fingers length exactly,' he said,

docking a tail with his sharp knife. Then we feasted.

We studied the weather, to know when we could go to pasture and when we must shelter.

'Red sky at night means pilgrim's delight,' said Jehan-Pastor, 'and a shepherd's.' But red sky in the morning and the bellwether reluctant to leave the barn, meant a day under cover. Sheep hate rain.

In June, the shearer called and the flock skipped in joy at the air on their flesh. I asked Mother why we had to bear our huge fur in summer heat.

'To protect us,' she told me. And she was right. Jehan-Pastor sought shade for the newly-fleeced sheep, wary of them turning sun-mad.

We spent summer up in the high pastures, not even going home to the barn at day's end. That's when our work really began, Mother's and mine, alert to any hint of predator, while Jehan-Pastou slept in his little hut. He stayed with us, rising early and always milking the ewes twice a day.

All through my first year Mother taught me what a pastou does. We marked our territory, as high on trees and bushes as we could manage, to show how big we were. We barked our loudest, 'No wolves, no bears, no foxes or dogs! No strangers! Don't come near.' And at night we watched the flocks, in case our warnings had been ignored. We were ready for all-comers.

Jehan-Pastor treated us the same way as he treated the shepherd boys and girls, who ran beside the flock, rounding up stragglers, while we led the way, our tails curved high like my master's crook. He would shout at us for wrong-doing just as he would fling earth with the scoop of his crook, to set sheep on the right path, but he was never cruel.

CHAPTER THREE

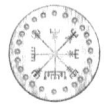

Together, Mother and I were invincible and how I wished her at my side when I faced the wolves of Montbrun. But let me enjoy the memory of happiness before telling of harder times.

In autumn we took the sheep to graze the stubble left from harvest, oats and wheat, each in turn. We moved them along the fields so that the following year's crop would benefit from the sheep droppings, nothing wasted. Autumn was the time of rain and hungry wolves so Jehan-Pastor was vigilant, as were we. He blocked the sheep's bells so that the wolves wouldn't know where to hide in the trees for a surprise attack.

Autumn was also a fruitful time. Ewes mated in September began to show if they carried young and must be treated gently.

Any sickness in a sheep was cured by cabbage diet or death, as the humours were too moist in autumn to risk any medicinal treatment for the mothers-to-be.

During my second winter, I grew a mane of dense fur and Jehan-Pastor said again, 'It is time.' He worked late in the evening on an iron hub, with holes. Into each hole he banged a flat-ended nail. He fitted the collar to my neck, a crown of outward-facing spikes. Whenever we went to the fields, I wore my collar, but no wolf came to test its spikes. My mother and I barked. Two pastous barking was enough to keep the wolves away and, in January, they were too busy with their own affairs to bother us. We heard their courtship calls echoing around the hills.

Jehan-Pastor loved his work and I thought he loved us. But, in the same way he split his sheep into wool and meat, stay and go, so he split Mother and me: she to stay and I to go. I do not hold that against him for no human could have brought me to adulthood with more care. And what Mother taught me was beyond price. I would miss them both.

What I didn't know then was that, like most good men, Jehan-Pastor saw no evil in others. When he looked at Malabric, he saw a shepherd, and to Jehan-Pastor, the shepherd's calling was ancient, sanctified and honourable.

A shepherd should never visit tavern, brothel or gambling-den. His only games should be hop-scotch or stick-and-ball, never dice. His life outdoors was a hymn to nature, suited to a pure heart.

This is a true description of Malabric's character exactly, only with every positive turned to negative and a heart as black as charcoal. But his appearance was the twin of Jehan-Pastor's, from his canvas smock and britches, under a waxed cape, to his leather gaiters made from old boots. He wore the plaited rope belt of his profession, hung with ointments, a knife, an awl, a needle-case and scissors.

His black felt hat was double-lined at front and back, but as I later found out, served to steal from his master. Like Jehan-Pastor, he stored wool clippings in the lining but he snipped and stole them whenever he could, to line his own nest. Jehan-Pastor only collected wool when a sheep had scabs or other infection and was clipped for treatment round a wound. At such a time, the precious clippings were stored and rendered in full, to the last hair, to Jehan-Pastor's liege lord.

Why do I go into such detail about this bad shepherd, whose very name fouls my mouth? Because Malabric came back from market with Jehan-Pastor, who had a new ram, a smile and the news that the ram's price was twelve breeding ewes and one young pastou – me.'

'The bad shepherd,' yipped the puppies, their voices high with excitement. Reymarca started chasing his tail.

'The bad shepherd,' agreed Nici and his growl rumbled through his young listeners, shaking the earth below their paws. He spat the name like poison. 'Malabric. Not worthy of being called Pastor.'

All the puppies mimicked Nici, spitting in pack solidarity, 'Malabric'. The adult dogs rose to their feet, stood guard, their eyes shining. Nici's mate and two of their full-grown offspring, bonded to the death.

'Malabric dragged me away from home, straining against the rope to see Mother, but she was shut in the barn with the sheep. I tried to reassure my little flock but I had so many questions. Who was my new master? Where were we going?'

'Malabric,' growled the puppies, making the sheep nearest them bleat and skitter away from the danger. Being sheep, they forgot within seconds that they'd been frightened.

Nici shook his great head. He must teach his pups to protect these silly creatures but it was not easy for him. He drew strength from his pack. Every dog had a story to tell and this was his, for better or worse. This part was for worse.

CHAPTER FOUR

'Malabric knew nothing of his own work, let alone ours. He'd nodded his head to all Pastor's counsel, and then brushed it off like dust. He treated me as he would any tool.

On the journey from home to my new domain of Montbrun, I came to hate the rope, which he sometimes used to hit me when I didn't understand what he wanted and sometimes used to keep me from straying. As if I'd leave those poor sheep alone with him! He ignored my warnings but I was too well brought up to bite him and merely ducked the lash when I could. If I'd known what was to come, I would not have held back.

What a walk that could have been with a different shepherd. A man who talked to me as we walked, who shared his dreams and his love of this outdoor life. A man who could see the subtle shift from grey to green as grass woke on the hillsides. A man who knew each sheep and called a halt for birthing, who travelled well and hale, instead of fast and crippling. A man who knew me and called me by my name. But I'd left any name with my brothers and sisters, in puppyhood. All I had now was 'pastou' and I held to that. I would be a good pastou, whatever happened.

Malabric removed the rope when we were far on our journey. He must have thought I'd stay with the flock, rather than run into a wilderness of shrub and stone, the vast unknown. He was right. But I did not stay from fear.

What the man did not do, my fellow-creatures did. The sheep from my home flock sniffed me, recognised me. I licked one's face and felt less lonely, although no sheep could replace Mother. When I thought of her, remembered all she had taught me of our duty, I held my head a little higher, as I walked my new path, leading the flock, while Malabric scooped clods of earth and flung them at stragglers.

I barked the ancient warning as we walked, my tongue already deep enough to keep bear, wolf and stray dog at bay. At least during day-time. Night belongs to its own creatures and, when most dogs sleep, we work hardest.

I knew I was fully accepted when I followed the birthing smell, the newborn cry, and the mother let me lick her lamb clean, dispose of debris that would attract wolves and stray dogs.'

Peldolce cleared her throat and Nici was reminded of his audience and his paternal duty.

'This will be part of your job, little ones,' he told his puppies, 'and you must learn what you may eat, and when. Mother and Jehan Pastor taught me well but there is no better pastou than *your* mother nor better shepherd than ours in Breyault. Watch and learn.'

'And the bravest of fathers.' Peldolce lifted her eyes to Nici's.

He couldn't meet her gaze, continued his tale instead. 'Looking after my ewes, I felt less lonely. Sometimes my tail would curve of its own accord into the arroundera plume of our kind, a feathery circle. My tail was happy.

One birth went badly and even Malabric knew he had to wait or he'd lose the mother. I licked the lamb clean but there was no bleat. I licked hard but there was nothing.

This was the first time I met a birth-death and I was confused. The lamb still smelled of birth and mother, as if life might come. But there was nothing. I turned away, my tail drooping.

'Eat it, you stupid dog,' snarled Malabric kicking the dead lamb nearer to me.

I couldn't. Not until its smell changed to meat. As you will find out, little ones, your nose will tell you when you may eat the dead of your flock. Until then, you must never draw blood from those you protect. You may play rough with each other and learn the consequences but not so much as one scratch is allowed on any of your flock or your people.'

'Nici dear,' interrupted Peldolce, 'we don't need to hear too much about stillborn lambs, not tonight... the puppies want to hear more about your adventures.'

Nici took the hint. 'So there were more than twelve sheep by the time we reached my new domain of Montbrun. Three pairs of twins had been born during our walk, sheep being given to twins.' He glared at Peldolce. 'I'm allowed to mention twins this night?'

'If you must.' Peldolce shook her shaggy head at the stupidity of males.

'Not that Malabric ever made a proper

tally of the flock. Jehan Pastor used to count the score and yell 'Tally,' notch his stick and then count again. Malabric threw some stones in his pocket and pretended that was his tally, if anybody asked him. He had to be more careful when the Lady of Montbrun started enquiring into the workings of her domain. Even then, he couldn't resist cheating. But manure floats and Malabric bobbed up every time he was pushed down.

He took us straight to the sheepfold, shut us in with the Montbrun flock and left. He couldn't wait to gamble at dice all he'd gained in market, would be my guess, from what I saw later. You can imagine how the Montbrun flock reacted to all these strangers! My ewes were protecting their lambs, the Montbrun ram was incensed at this invasion and I didn't know what to do to calm them all down.

I tried to let the ram sniff me but I had to duck his horns and growl a warning when he was offensive to my ewes. The moment I growled, all the Montbrun sheep bleated themselves into a panic and the whole ritual started all over again. Suspicion, butting, calm, sniffing, fear. That was a long night, the different factions skittering behind food troughs, my ewes in a miserable huddle.

Finally, morning came, a very late

morning and a shepherd who smelled like a newly fertilised field of young spelt. He forgot to change the water and brought no food for me but at least we got out of the stifling atmosphere to the open fields.

Tempers calmed with space and good grazing. I encouraged sniffing, and put up with some rough treatment, in the interests of harmony, for my ewes' sake. I didn't growl once although I was sorely provoked, and my reward was the peaceful bleating of sheep. Not that Malabric noticed my work. He slept all day.

By the time we reached the summer pastures, I cared about the whole flock – *my* flock – and did my duty by them. I was still young and felt the morning wildness and the twilight fight against my inner wolf. I missed the company of my kind and would sometimes forget that sheep had neither speed in running nor agility in twisting, to duck my jaws, open in play. You can imagine the beatings I took if Malabric saw my gambols.

Summer pasture was lush and open. I inspected the perimeter. Plenty of rocks that would hide wolves but no cover for bear. Night would be the only cover that might stretch my senses. Though Mother and I worked hard, we were also lucky. At least three protection dogs are needed to be sure of defence. The Lords of Breyault know this.' Nici nodded his great head at the adults in the barn.

'You know how we work, covering each other and the flock. Imagine me, young, alone on a hillside with only a strange man to help me. I allowed myself a short nap, but must have dropped too deep asleep, exhausted from doing three dogs' work, so young. When I awoke, I was alone on the hillside with my flock of sheep. The shepherd had gone.

That night was the longest of my life. I jumped at every night-bird's call. When I heard wolves howl, I worried in case they were nearer than I thought, and circling. What could one pastou do? But the night passed without incident and I came to accept the terrible burden placed on my young shoulders, just as the ewes put up with erratic milking. What choice did we have? Malabric left the sheep whenever he could, slipping back to the chateau and his dissolute ways.

CHAPTER FIVE

As I grew older, I missed rough games less but my working partnerships more, both with Mother and with Jehan Pastor. Being sole dog of a lazy shepherd ate away at my flesh, which was already weakened by random feeding.

From my straw bed, surrounded by sheep, I could hear dogs barking at the chateau, so close but barred to me. One day's end, when we led the sheep home to the barn, I hung back, camouflaged by the flock, and while Malabric took the stones out of his pocket to show anybody watching that he counted the sheep, I bounded towards the happy barks.

I didn't find any other pastous but all kinds of hounds greeted me with tail – or teeth – in the chateau courtyard. My politeness soon disarmed those who felt threatened by my appearance and I was able to roll a few in the dust, to our mutual pleasure. My flock would be safe enough in the barn for the night and I needed company and food.

Sure enough, my new friends led me into the Great Hall. I copied their behaviour, ignoring curses and rushing past men's boots and ladies' slippers to find a spot under a trestle table. When a velvet sleeve dipped below the table and a hand emerged, waved a meaty bone, I hesitated. This was too good to be true. Malabric had tested me this way and beaten me when I took the bone. The bone waggled again and I was pushed aside by a black and tan scent hound, with ears that almost touched the floor. He grabbed the bone and lay, chewing beside me, under the table.

Before my hunger could provoke me to fight for the bone, another hand appeared beside my nose, waved a half-eaten bone and this time I didn't hesitate. We lay there, the hound and I, gnawing. Life was good here. I gorged on meat and marrow until my belly was warm. The Lord and Lady of Montbrun filled their hall with light and laughter, or so I thought then. Later, I realised that the Lord of Montbrun was a shadow-man, empty of all that a man should be, and Costansa, his Lady, was what made him so.

That first time, I sensed only a home, a life I yearned for. A girl sang and made music, while the murmur of human voices showed approval. I had forgotten the sound of approval and I let that too fill me with warmth, as if it was meant for me.

I was a protection dog and for too long I'd been protecting myself as well as my flock. The sweet voice of the girl slipped under my guard, reminded me of my puppyhood and my hopes. Maybe, I thought, maybe there could be a warm-belly feeling between a man and a dog, or between a girl and a dog.

I slept under a tree near the barn and slipped among the sheep when Malabric let them out in the morning. I pranced at the front as if I'd been with the flock the whole time, my tail in a high arroundera. I worked that day with good cheer because I knew that I would eat well and have good company in the evening, whatever my shepherd made me suffer in between. And he always made me suffer.

He yelled commands I didn't understand, though I could tell from how he shouted that he wanted me to do something. Beatings followed. I shook off his orders like water-drops, even when I learned what they meant. How can we do our work if we obey those who have no sense of danger? Especially those who have no love either. The beatings left their mark.

Sometimes, our paths would cross those of another shepherd, another flock and another dog. Though they worked as pastous, they were brindled, brown and black, never white-furred like me. We were too protective of our flocks to drop our guard and play but our masters enjoyed breaking bread and talking, while we dogs lay watchful. One of these men reminded me of Jehan-Pastor, a warmth in his voice as he spoke, even to his dog, who looked to his master as much as to his sheep.

This master, Gaudis, even played a game with his dog while they were resting. He rolled up a hunk of bread in cloth and threw this round for the dog to catch, which was done without the object touching the ground. Instead of tearing into the cloth and devouring the bread, as I would have done, the dog brought the cloth ball to his shepherd and the game began again. After several repetitions, Gaudis opened up the cloth and gave the dog the bread, with praise.

'You'll spoil him,' grunted Malabric.

'I'm training him,' was the reply.

'This is all you need to train a dog.' Malabric shook his crook and I crouched, ears low, awaiting the blow. 'See. He knows a dog's place.'

The other man's lips set tight but all he said was, 'The ewes are past milking now but I like your plan for next year. You make good cheese. There's five of us will send you two buckets of milk each week from March till August. We've a trustworthy waggoner will do the round, for one cheese in payment. He'll carry other goods when he can to make it worth his while.

Malabric pursed his lips. 'One bucket will make four cheeses.' He picked up a stick and notched a tally of four, five times. 'So you shall have twenty cheeses each month but give me one for the making of it.'

Gaudis frowned as he puzzled out the counting. 'That's more than fair,' he agreed. 'Each of us shall lose one cheese each month for five months and in August we shall draw straws to decide who must lose one more. We are in agreement and I give you my word.'

'As I give mine that I shall make you the finest cheese this side of Carcassonne. You could sell it at market and make good coin.'

Gaudis looked shocked. 'But the cheeses belong to my Lord, as do the sheep.'

'Of course, of course,' Malabric hastened to right his mistake. 'I spoke in jest.'

Gaudis was indeed like Jehan. He saw no evil.

'How foolish of me to think otherwise!' Both men smiled at a good bargain well made. Gaudis drew the pipes out of his belt and played a merry tune, the music of lambs skipping in sunshine, the joy of a shepherd's life. Such moments were rare.

Like Malabric, I tried to get back to the chateau whenever I could. But, unlike him, I made sure I could safely leave my flock. At first, I would only slip away on the occasional evening and night, when the sheep were in the barn. But when I stayed locked in with the flock, I dreamed of meaty bones, human laughter and soft voices that reminded me of Jehan Pastor, the soft nuzzle of a fellow-being, and I woke drooling, alone. No matter how many sheep were on Malabric's tally, I felt alone. Maybe he was right when he told everybody I was a useless dog. Worse than useless, after Black Winter.

A dog's like his master, they say, and Malabric was the worst of shepherds. In May he sheared the sheep himself but pretended he'd hired a man, so he could keep the payment. And it was the breeding ewes, yearlings and lambs that paid most dearly. I licked their cuts, where blood beaded on nicked flesh. If he hadn't washed them before shearing, the lambs wouldn't have frisked so much, shaking the water from their ears, and he'd have had a better hold on their tied legs. Which were tied too tight.

He took no care to keep the newly-fleeced flock sheltered from mid-day sun and some took ill with heat. I was glad of my thick fur as sometimes the nearest shade was miles out of reach. Not that sheep had the sense to seek shade. That's why they needed their shepherd's care – and mine. And I was weary of thinking for a flock of sheep, who could not think for themselves.

High summer was tiring. Malabric left us out in the fields, night after night, while he went back to the chateau. I worked. Hungry, lonely, dreaming of the Great Hall, I never left my flock and no harm came to them. I grew thin but I carried on working.

When he ran out of the money he'd made from stolen wool, Malabric stayed for days with the flock. He took the sharp knife from his belt and cut some of the fattest ewes. Not like Jehan-Pastor had done, to bleed a sick animal from its muzzle and make it better. Not even as Malabric usually did to treat an animal, cutting its ears. Jehan-Pastor said a sheep without ears is without honour and only a bad shepherd would draw blood this way. As if I needed any more evidence that Malabric was a bad shepherd! No, this time, my master was cutting bits of fat out of the ewes he'd selected.

And he was smiling. 'Will fetch a pretty penny for tallow,' he said. And then he was gone, to collect and spend the proceeds, while the ewes he'd wounded grew thin and ill. I comforted them as best I could but my heart bounded after Malabric to the chateau, away from these miserable sheep and my miserable work to life, laughter and a full belly.

I carried on working.

Then one day, things changed. Malabric rushed up the hill to the flock, threw me bread from his panier and leaned on his crook, every inch the picture of a dutiful shepherd watching his flock. Only his heavy breathing and sour smell told a different tale.

Shortly afterwards, Costansa, the Lady of Montbrun, followed in Malabric's footsteps, marched up the hill and approached the flock, who bleated and jittered.

'You do me honour, my Lady,' my master grovelled.

'I am taking stock of my Lord's domain and wish a full report on his flocks.'

Whether it was some wisps of wool poking out from the pouch in his hat, or his manner in tallying, something about her shepherd left the Lady cold and suspicious.

'My Lord has no knowledge of sheep-keeping, Malabric, but I know every aspect of a crook and I am watching you closely,' were her parting words, as she turned on her heel.

My master said nothing but until the season of leaf-fall, he was careful to give no cause for complaint. The barn was mucked out, fresh straw laid and the manger filled with hay. He took us back there most days, or left us in pastures with shade, and near a brook. He gave us clean water daily, fed me my crust of bread and used a switch to drive the sheep or chastise me, rather than the crook, which I had come to loathe. We were all in better health from this care. We needed to be. The season of the wolf was upon us.'

CHAPTER SIX

'Our work, as shepherd and as pastou, follows the yearly weather rhythms of sky and pasture; of tupping and birth; of nurture, harvest and death; and also the hunger patterns of our enemies, in their own seasons of rut and glut. No time of year is without danger but we learn when to be most watchful, and for what. Our mad brothers, errant dogs, are tempted most by lambs in springtime, as are those who swoop from the skies and carry off newborns in their fierce talons. Lumbering bears seek easy pickings of any size, raiding in the fog of high summer pastures. They stay on the heights and gorge in early autumn, before their big sleep, when we are safe from them. Vile creatures, they eat without killing, and they kill by mistake. Whole flocks of frightened sheep can run off cliffs.

Our grey cousins will stalk the flock in any month, hoping to snatch and steal. Their jaws are strong enough to take a lamb and run. One wolf is no match for a pastou and even a pack looks for unguarded prey. My barking warned them off all summer. I didn't see one slinking shadow while I kept watch at night. Nor bear nor wolf braved the many beasts I pretended to be through night echoes and movement.

But when November mists hung in the valleys, shrouding every tree in ghosts, the wolves came down to the lower pastures with us. Grey as rain clouds, I could scent them stalking, restless, hungry. Ready to take risks.

Malabric's temper fed on the evil autumn humours, cold and contagious. Of all weathers, sheep hate wet and cold, so it was doubly important that they were shepherded into the barn each night and kept there if the weather boded ill. I stayed with them, ignoring the lure of a sweet voice in my head, singing of meat bones and warmth.

Not so Malabric, who gambled at night, rose late, red-eyed as any wolf. He took the sheep to graze as near the barn as could be found a hint of stubble and he rushed off to squander time with his cronies at the chateau. The ewes were mated, needed no milking and he saw no reason to keep sheep company. Or me.

In the bare, leached fields, I tried to bark the warnings Mother taught me but my stomach growled louder than I could and the trees, swathed in dripping white, muffled my voice.

Each day, I saw grey shadows moving through the trees, flickering in the corner of my eyes. When I chased them, they were gone, creatures of my imagination. I raced round the flock, marking our territory, but the boundary wavered in the mist, interrupted by trees that seemed to loom ever closer.

The wolves had their pack. I had no-one but my sheep. 'Baaa,' they said.

It was a sheep who gave the alert when the attack happened. A ewe screamed death from the other side of the flock, behind me. The enemy had struck, one luring me to this place while others circled round. I could not be in both places! I carved a path to the scream, directly through the huddled sheep as they bleated their fear. When I reached the scream, I realised how much difference a pack made.

A group of ewes had been separated from their fellows, herded towards a copse, where they could be harried from different directions. Some were dead, some dying or under attack from lithe shapes with dripping jaws.

I roared my fury and launched myself at the nearest wolf. Taken unawares, he soon reddened the fleece below him from his ripped throat but I was too late. His pack dissolved in the grey, materialising one at a time behind me or to the side as I whirled, chasing an invisible enemy. Snarling, biting, I used teeth, claws and the spikes on my collar, while my ears rang with bleats as my sheep died.

I was still whirling when the absence struck me. It was over. The pack had gone. The wolves I'd killed lay beside the dead sheep. That's when the full horror struck me. All the dead sheep were from Jehan-Pastor's flock, my special ewes, my first flock. That's why the wolves had separated them off so easily. The Montbrun flock never fully accepted the newcomers and, under threat of wolves, the herd had looked to itself. A herd is not a pack.

I lay down, bloodied muzzle on ripped, red claws and I waited. In case the wolves returned. If Malabric thought I was sleeping when he saw me amid the dead, he was wrong. If he thought I'd forgotten the living, maybe, there, he had touched on a truth. My sheep were dead and it was my fault. There is no worse dishonour.

I didn't even feel the crook when Malabric hit me for letting the wolves among the sheep. No punishment he gave could earn pardon for my failure. He removed the spiked iron collar that I wore when working outdoors and he never fastened it on me again. Maybe he sold it. All I know is that I felt heavier without Jehan-Pastor's gift.

When I licked my wounds among the flock in the barn that night, I thought my life was over. But even in that darkest hour, I was haunted by memory of sweet song, of a hand coming below the table, of a caress. Such a small thing to cling to, hope.'

CHAPTER SEVEN

'I spent winter licking my wounds and ducking Malabric's blows. His rough indifference had turned putrid, a boil that could only be lanced by my death. And I deserved his hatred.

I carried on working but when I looked at the sheep, I saw my dead ewes. When I looked at trees, I saw thousands of wolves, all lean and lethal. I could not stomach the flock's stupidity. I preferred to confront wolves, imaginary or real, and I set myself the task of marking every tree, every blade of grass. Of barking strength and defiance. Of rushing at the densest patch of fog, the blackest darkness. Nobody would see my fear. Least of all me.

But I could not face the vacuous nature of sheep. They baaed and bleated as if nothing had happened. Their eyes reflected chewed cud. They would skip over my dead body as easily as off a cliff, frightened and headlong, following a crazed leader. They were not my kind but this work was my doom and I accepted it.

At first, I was too ashamed to return to the Great Hall but when I heard the lilt of a girl's voice as we went into the barn late one evening, I veered away from the flock and was running to the chateau before Malabric could catch me. And so it began again, my evenings under the table and my days protecting a flock I no longer cared about.

Each night I slept outdoors, my thick white coat all the blanket I needed, even when winter's thick white coat covered the ground. I was less lonely under a tree near the barn, alone, than I was in the warm straw with the sheep. Each morning, I blended with the flock as Malabric let them out, and he was none the wiser. We were both bad shepherds.

There is comfort in having your own place, even under a table, and the long-eared hound welcomed me back. He knew nothing of my failure, which gave me comfort of a different kind. Maybe, in different company, I could be the dog I'd always meant to be.

Humans too had their own places and I

recognised the hands, sleeves and smells that visited me with leftovers. One hand was special, work-hardened, with oil and soot in the creases, however much scrubbed and overlain with tallow and lye scent. He also smelled of steel, smoke and horses. A smith? But there was leather and straw too, kitchen smells and strewing herbs, as if he walked the whole chateau in his work. All-trades man? He hummed gently when the girl sang, was loud in his praise when she finished. Her friend. Though she sat at another table, with the Lord and Lady.

'Just like her mother,' he said, his voice proud, as if she was his good puppy. He stretched down under the table, just as I reached up in hope of food, and he caught the side of my cheek, caressed me. Stroked me again, so I knew he meant it.

'Why there you are, big boy,' he murmured. I hadn't been touched like that since Jehan-Pastor. I trembled but stayed put, heard only sweet song, felt only a caress. There were no dying sheep in the Great Hall. I thought no evil could enter such a place. Like Jehan-Pastor and Gaudis, I too was still innocent.

One night, when I sneaked off to my sleeping-place, two voices in the darkness made me stop short. Lady Costansa and

Malabric. I didn't want to be caught so I waited in the shadows.

'I warned you,' the lady growled. 'You should be hanged for any one of these crimes against my Lord. I have kept a fine record. A fat ewe sold at market and replaced by a thin one, stolen no doubt – though your tally is so miscounted nobody would notice one missing sheep! Twenty ewes killed by wolves and yet my men saw only ten bodies, not fresh. You say the wolves dragged ten away. Yet that dog of yours killed three wolves and was guarding the flock as best he could. I say you took ten of your Lord's sheep and made profit. Do I need to go on?'

Malabric fawned. 'There is an explanation for all of this my Lady. I am not to blame. The market-seller lied to you and you are mistaken in the dog. He is vicious and it was he who joined the wolves in savaging the twenty sheep. I pray you, let me restore your good opinion of me, by whatever means.'

'There might be a way…'

Malabric's eyes smiled in the moonlight, and he bared his teeth, as when he made the cheese deal with Gaudis, yet to be completed. 'Anything, my Lady.'

'The girl is an irritation. My Lord will

never forget his first wife with a daughter who grows more like her mother every day she blossoms. I want rid of her.'

There was a silence, full of darkness. 'Rid of her, my Lady?'

'Spare me the details. You've made enough sheep disappear. There are wolves round here. There are villains with knives, who prey on young girls. Especially a young girl who ventures into the forest sometimes. Just make certain.'

'Yes, my Lady. Give me till springtime, when we are outdoors more.'

'Till springtime,' she conceded. 'We understand each other and the fewer who see us together, the better.'

She lifted her gown above the dirt and headed back towards the Great Hall, while my master stood, pensive. Then he turned the other way and I was free to curl up in my usual place, undisturbed except by my thoughts.

I'd recognised the words 'that dog', and their tone. I'd been sold once. Maybe I'd be sold again, although I was no longer worth a fine ram but merely a good kicking. My master said so. No, whatever was planned for 'that dog' would be worse than I endured now. Eventually, I went to sleep and the year continued its indifferent course.

Days lightened earlier, lambs were born. When they were strong and skipping, in the skittish way of the young, my master set to work in earnest, milking their mothers before going to pasture and again in the evenings. Each day, he sent some buckets of milk to the chateau and kept some for cheese-making. And, of course, for his own sustenance. But not for mine. I'd licked the whey-bucket once, when he was distracted and the taste, salty and sour, made sheep more tolerable.

We were outside more as the weather improved and I followed him, curious, to his hut. There, he added something to the milk, then heated it over in a large pot over the fire, until it clumped, when he hung it in a cloth to drain over a bucket. He squeezed the hanging cloth until it was a ball shape, which he stored on a shelf.

Gaudis kept his word and the five shepherds sent their pails of milk with the waggoner once a week. We had to wait for the delivery before we could go to pasture and I watched my master check under the lid of each container to see that he'd not been cheated. When he was satisfied, he'd hand the agreed number of finished cheeses to the waggoner, to be distributed. I knew he sent cheeses to the chateau, from the Montbrun flock's milk. But I was surprised that he tucked away a cheese each week, in a box under his straw mattress.

'Market in May,' he said. 'Do the Lady's work first, then make myself scarce at the sheepmart, while there's a hullabaloo. Might even get rid of that useless dog to some fool, get me a proper one.'

My tail drooped. Every time he mentioned me, I was reminded of my failure. He pointed to me when our paths crossed those of the other shepherds and he made the gesture I'd seen when he swapped a sheep for a new knife. An old ewe past bearing, though she was shown with weaned twin lambs when Malabric bartered her away. He made sure to test the knife's blade. Maybe the shepherds remembered that swap when they shook their heads at me and walked on.'

CHAPTER EIGHT

'Then came the day that smelled wrong. Malabric had been tense, on edge for days, holding his knife and muttering to himself, then sheathing it again. 'Maybe tomorrow,' he kept saying.

It was milk delivery day but the waggoner's face looked more curdled than hot cheese-pots and three shepherds threw the canvas open and jumped out of the covered wagon.

'Good-day, Malabric, said Gaudis, polite but cold. 'We wanted to see how our cheeses are made. Filipot and Otz couldn't manage to come but they know we are here.'

'I don't have much time. You should have let me know you were coming.' Malabric, curt without offence, as a busy man might be. 'But of course you can see your cheeses – and take them back with you.' He hefted the buckets out of the wagon and the other shepherds helped him carry them into the hut.

I watched. My master pointed to the pot, the cloths, the cheeses hanging, the finished cheeses on the shelf. His mouth, hands and body moved a lot but his eyes kept flicking the other way, to his hidey-hole.

The other shepherds relaxed, showed interest, nodded satisfaction at their cheeses, finished and in the making. They accepted the invitation to crouch together, shepherd-style, and sup from a bowl of whey, sharing amicably.

I moved closer, wondering whether I might win another lick of salty cream taste and I automatically ducked the whack on the nose aimed by Malabric.

'That dog follows you everywhere,' commented Gaudis

'You want him, you can have him,' my master said, his voice dripping contempt. 'You could teach him to play fetch.'

They both looked at me. I heard the word 'fetch' and wagged my tail. If I pleased Gaudis, maybe he would take me as his dog. Maybe I could make a fresh start.

I knew that 'fetch' meant 'Get that cloth ball and bring it to me.' So I did. Eager to make a good impression on Gaudis, I raced to the cot, scrabbled out the straw before my master could stop me, clawed the wooden box open and took one of the cloth balls delicately in my teeth. I ignored the tempting smell of cheese that pervaded my nostrils – if only I had the dulled senses of humans! – and I dropped the fetched cheese in Gaudis's open hands.

Then pandemonium broke out. All the men jumped to their feet and shouted at each other while I backed away, uncertain what was going on or who to chastise. Was this a dispute over leadership?

Two men held Malabric while the others pulled the damaged box out from under the cot and extricated the remaining cheeses, shouting.

'You *have* been diddling us!'

'Selling our cheeses!'

'How many have you stolen each month? Each week!'

'It's all a misunderstanding!' My master's voice barely rose over the hubbub but I heard his wheedling tone.

'Let's take him to the Lord. He'll hang for this!'

'Yes, take me to the Lord and I can explain,' Malabric pleaded.

'I don't trust him,' said the black-browed shepherd and the others nodded. 'He has some way of getting the Lord on his side. A man like him slithers like a snake.'

'The Lord don't interfere in shepherds' business if we don't ask him. Let's deal with him ourselves.'

'We can't hang him like he deserves or the Lord won't like us carrying out his justice.'

They mused on the matter while Malabric struggled to get out of the strong grasp in which he was now held.

'Toss him in a blanket,' suggested Gaudis.

Malabric went white. 'No,' he gasped.

The shepherds conferred.

'An he breaks a leg, who cares.'

'An he dies of the infection, that would be a sorry fate, wouldn't it.'

'Agreed!' Smug as cats, the shepherds carried Malabric out of the hut, still protesting. I followed a little way but then made the second of that day's fateful decisions. Why should I follow Malabric? Why should I call him master? He'd lost in the fight for leadership. Gaudis didn't want me.

I turned back to the hut and licked out the pot of whey before heading to the chateau. There, I made my introduction to every dog I'd not met before and I played with those I liked. I was a bad pastou, a bad dog. Then I might as well live down to my reputation.

When my playmates headed for the Great Hall at the end of the day, I went with them, hoping to add meat and bread to my earlier portion of whey. I found my usual table and company, sniffed a greeting, then stared fixedly at the underside of the table, willing a hand to appear.

Not only did the hand of all-trades man fulfil my hopes, but he passed an entire trencher to me under the table, meaty stew *and* the bread on which it was served. The man had not eaten one mouthful. What an amazing day this was!

My only disappointment was that the girl did not perform. I missed her music and her voice, so I tuned in straight away when I heard her tones next to all-trades man, a fleeting whisper. Meadow-flower girl scent flared my nostrils.

'Thank you,' she said. 'I owe you my life.'

'Go with God, my Lady Roxane. May we meet again in better times.'

'I hope so, Gilles.'

Their urgency was unsettling but I had gravy to lick so I concentrated on that until I saw the man's legs straighten, move away from the table. Nobody else was leaving.

Quite the opposite. A man had started singing, clanging like a deep bell, not pleasant to my ears, although his audience seemed to like him well enough. Perhaps he was higher in their pack than they were.

The wrongness scent filled me again, now I was full-bellied and irritated by the entertainment. I extricated myself from the table, from the hall, and in the twilight I saw a man walking away from the chateau towards the woods. *Gilles*, was my first thought. *Wolves*, my second. Even though it was springtime, grey shadows were never far from my mind.

I followed Gilles, observed his strange behaviour from a safe distance. He checked that nobody was watching. They were all in the Hall. He carried a sack and a shoe, and bent low at every pace, touching the ground. As he continued this halting progress, along a path into the trees, I sniffed the track he'd left.

Gilles' prints were deep in the damp soil, with what smelled like a second person's track beside them. Meadow-flower girl scent with sweat, in two places. I puzzled over the tracks. Roxane had been this way, walking close to Gilles' tracks. She wasn't with him now but there was her smell, in his steps.

Then I understood. The shoe was Roxane's and Gilles had been dragging it along the ground. I palpated my dewlaps to get the air scents, ignoring all-trades man and girl smells to identify bloody meat. My table-mate of the long ears would have been proud of me.

I loped after Gilles, following him more closely among the trees, stifling the temptation to bark warning. This was not my usual kind of guard duty but something was wrong. I did not believe that Gilles had hurt Roxane. Not when I'd heard the affection in their voices. But why was he making scents that told a story of violence?

I tracked him into the woods to a crossing of paths. I watched from behind a tree, like the wolf-cousin I was. He'd stopped and was staring at the ground where the most-trodden path turned left. Then he looked closely at the trees around him. A piece of cloth had snagged on a branch. He removed this, stashed it in his sack and took out some scraps of meat. These, he buried under the surface at the start of a narrow path heading right, using Roxane's shoe to push them into the soil. He dragged the shoe along the ground into the untrodden woods, then returned for a final look at the scene. He kicked earth onto the path that turned left, then threw some twigs and small stones onto it. Then he set off in the opposite direction, breaking branches whether they were in his way or not, as he went deeper into the forest.

I investigated. First, the area where Gilles had laid scent. That was easy enough as I had seen him place girl-shoe-scent and meat, then make his own heavy-footed way. More interesting was the path where he'd covered up scents. I sniffed, palpated, tasted the air. There was no question. Roxane had gone this way.

I stood at the crossing of paths in the forest and my final choosing was upon me. A good pastou would return to his sheep, would not have left them in the first place. I was not that dog. Some harm was in the air, some invisible wolf, and my instinct was to protect a sweet-voiced girl. No rope, no crook was there to stop me.

Why was Gilles laying tracks, with meat smells? To be followed of course, by my long-eared friend and his like.

If the scent-hound followed in my footsteps, he would easily sniff the full story, including my part in it but he didn't have to tell. Not if I left a message. I peed long and full at the start of Roxane's path. 'I was here. I will follow the girl. Leave this to me. I have it under control. Goodbye.' I told my friend. He would understand.

Then off I went, crashing through the undergrowth, heedless of the tracks I left. Nobody was looking for me. Trees opened up into vineyards. Although her scent was clear, the girl was nowhere to be seen. I trusted my nose, followed it towards the boundary where field met a path as broad as a river.

And there, in a ditch, Roxane lay sleeping, in coarse clothing that would barely keep her warm. I eased myself in behind her, lay stretched out to warm her as I had newborn lambs, in the time when I wanted nothing more than to be a good pastou. This was what I was born for, and that night, I felt her breathe between my paws, her skin like shorn ewe against my fur. I gave her my warmth and a promise I will never break. She gave me purpose and a second chance. I would lay down my life for her in a heartbeat.

The next morning she looked at me with a stranger's eyes. She named herself Estela and she called me Nici but her bitterness when she called me 'Stupid' was aimed at herself.

We would travel a long road together, with many adventures but I will never forget the first time we stood shoulder to shoulder, defying the world. Beside that very ditch.'

'Tell us about Lord Dragonetz,' asked Reymarca, scratching behind his ear. 'How fierce he was.'

'How brave.'

'How fine in his armour and with his shining sword,' the puppies clamoured.

Nici opened his mouth to speak but the storm's sudden howl drowned him out and as the shriek died away, an unexpected threat made all the dogs bark. Someone was hammering on the door.

CHAPTER NINE

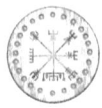

'Musca! Are you in there?'

The dogs stood down at the familiar voice and the little boy rubbed sleepy eyes, removed himself from the warm pile of puppies.

'I'm coming Papa. Let me unlock the door.'

With a flurry of snowflakes, a tall man in woollen cloak entered the sheepfold, swept Musca up in his arms and swung him laughing in the air. A patterned sword of Damascene steel flashed beneath the swirling cloak.

'I'm a big boy now,' Musca objected.

'And a heavy one. I'm training with weights,' Lord Dragonetz teased. 'I shall kill Raoulf for leaving you. I've been worried sick!'

Suddenly serious, the boy insisted on

standing to face his father. 'If there was any fault, it was mine, Sire. Raoulf thought I was asleep and our men wished advice on the eastern defences. Perhaps I should have gone instead of Raoulf, as you were occupied? I am never sure how much I should represent you in your absence.'

'No, you were right to allow Raoulf to go,' Dragonetz told Musca, 'and I must say your mother has given you a very impressive vocabulary.'

'Thank you, Sire.' Musca's lips trembled. 'How is my lady Mother.'

Dragonetz could not hold back his joy and swept up his son once more. 'She is well, well, well! And you have a baby sister! We shall ring all the bells in the morning.'

'Shall I like having a baby sister?'

His father's answer was interrupted by a streak of white, rushing past Dragonetz through the open barn door to join his mistress.

'Find Estela, Nici!' Dragonetz did not usually give redundant orders but nobody would prevent Nici joining his mistress now, just as he had on Musca's birth-day.

The puppies looked round-eyed at the open door, where flurries of snow still whirled. Their mother sighed and licked them.

'That's your father, through and through,' she murmured.

'That's Nici, through and through.' Dragonetz shook his head. 'He'll see your sister before you do! Hop on my back and I'll carry you.'

'I already have brothers and sisters,' declared Musca, turning to bid farewell. 'Night night, woof, woof. They speak to me, Papa. They tell me stories.'

Dragonetz smoothed an unruly lock of black hair out of his son's eyes. 'On Christmas Eve at midnight all beasts speak, or so they say. In memory of a stable and the birth of a child. Maybe you're the lucky one and you heard them.'

'I did. I'm lucky! But I think they speak always and we only hear them on Christmas Eve. Will she fight with me?'

Dragonetz was wise enough to realise this was a hope not a fear.

'She needs to grow a bit first. But if she's like her mother, I think she will make a good sparring-partner. Until then, you must be her protector.'

'Like Nici.'

'Yes, like Nici. Someone she can look up to.'

If you enjoyed this book,
please share your thoughts in a review,
however short.
Reviews help other readers find my books.

Anyone who reviews one of my books
can have their dog featured in
the Readers' Dogs Hall of Fame
on my website.

Contact me at jeangill.com
I love to hear from readers.

ACKNOWLEDGMENTS

Many thanks to:–
all my readers, especially *The Troubadours* fan who told me she'd love to know Nici's story;
my editor and friend, Lesley Geekie;
Babs, Claire, Karen, Kristin and Jane for their friendship, support and critical input;

John N. Green, University of Bradford, for his patience with questions like 'Did Occitan shepherds have a counting system like 'Yan, tan, tethera' (Northern English)'? That hare is still running but the chase has been fun (for me);

and Matthieu Mauriès, shepherd, goatherd and breeder of Great Pyrenees. His facebook account of his life in the Pyrenees, and photos of his dogs at work, presents the reality of rural living: sometimes beautiful and sometimes heart-wrenching, always back-breaking – some things don't change across the centuries.

Two sources I drew on heavily, both in French, were:
Le Montagne de Pyrénées – Matthieu Mauriès available from the *Hogan des Vents website*
Le Bon Berger: Le Vray Regime Et Gouvernement Des Bergers Et Bergeres – Jehan de Brie

AUTHOR'S NOTE

When I asked fans what untold story they would like to read from the 12th century world of *The Troubadours Quartet*, the first suggestion to hit me as a 'must-write' was the story of Nici. Many readers have told me that Nici, the Great Pyrenees, is a favourite character. His role in the adventures of Estela and Dragonetz is crucial but gets few lines, so it was a pleasure to slip into a dog's point of view and give Nici his due.

Having been owned by six Great Pyrenees over the course of forty years, I know and love this wonderful breed. When I wrote *Someone to Look Up To*, I found it easy to slip into the voice of Sirius, who sees dog training from the dog's point of view. Some say I've never really returned to human. But *Nici's Tale* required knowledge of medieval shepherding as well as dogs, so I set to work on the research.

Thanks to Matthieu Mauriès and other modern French breeders of Great Pyrenees, I'm well-read on the current use and training of protection dogs. The recent reintroduction of wolves and bears in southern France has led to violent disputes between environmentalists and farmers. It has also led to increasing use of protection dogs, especially Great Pyrenees. During the fifteen years I've lived in rural Drome Provencale, I've seen signs popping up on farmland, warning ramblers how to behave faced with a *patou* (the nickname for a Great Pyrenees, derived from the even older word *pastou*).

The dogs' courageous behaviour when faced with bears, wolves or other predators can be seen in many home videos on youtube and it is obvious that one dog cannot be effective. If you watch three patous working together against a wolf pack, you can only admire their intelligence, night vision, collaboration and sheer guts. Yet, for economic reasons, or from ignorance, young dogs are still left alone to protect flocks, as was Nici.

Armed with an understanding of the patou's work and modern training, I did my

AUTHOR'S NOTE

research to find out what was different in medieval times and grew very excited at finding a treatise on good shepherding, written by a medieval French shepherd, Jehan de Brie. I relied heavily on Jehan for details but was sorry to be forced by storytelling priorities to omit all the wonderful details of sheep diseases and treatments, and the hilarious account of his career, from letting the pigs run amok to being laid up for months by a kick from a cow. These made for wonderful monologues at breakfast as I bored my husband to tears with Jehan's latest disaster. Although Jehan lived in the 14th century not the 12th, and in northern France rather than Occitania, shepherding did not change much and the authenticity of the account made it perfect background material for my story.

So, how was medieval shepherding different from modern? My first surprise was that there were, apparently, no herding-dogs. Collies as a breed did not exist. A shepherd had one mastiff to protect the flocks and the training methods used on Nici were those recommended by Jehan, unlikely to achieve very much with a Great Pyrenees, in my judgement. However, the instinct of these dogs to protect those (sheep or people) they've bonded with, is so strong

AUTHOR'S NOTE

that they will usually do their work regardless of training.

In *Song Hereafter: 1154 in Hispania and the Isles of Albion*, I mention Pembroke herding-dogs, better known today as Pembrokeshire corgis. The breed did indeed exist in the 12th century and they are a herding breed, so my theory is that *some* farmers discovered and made use of the skills of such dogs, when herding cattle or sheep. Maybe this began in Pembroke, a small county in Wales – who knows! So far, I haven't found any corroboration and collies don't appear until several centuries later.

Instead of herding sheepdogs, there were children. Wanna-be shepherds and shepherdesses would run beside the flock, even stay out in the fields. There was no shortage of people for the most menial of jobs and the smallest reward. 'Childhood' was a time of apprenticeship and Musca would indeed have learned the longbow at seven, and started training as a squire, then a knight. When he speaks, he mixes formal adult language with a child's understanding and this seems to me to fit a noble's son, especially when on best behaviour. There are many examples of aristocratic children writing in adult style, sometimes with a more age-appropriate drawing alongside the text.

Another aspect of Jehan's treatise is the sacred nature of shepherding and he quotes Bible scripture again and again, proud of being a shepherd. The status of shepherding in medieval Christendom was that of an honourable vocation. It is no coincidence that *pastor* (shepherd) came to mean a Christian minister, in charge of his metaphorical flock.

The notion of 'a good shepherd' had spiritual and metaphorical resonance, recognized by peasant and lord alike. Equally, a 'bad shepherd' was worse than any shoddy worker. Sheep-stealing was a heinous crime, not just because it was theft but because it was an attack on a shepherd. Malabric, the bad shepherd in my story, is punished in the manner decreed in the *Second Shepherds' Play* of *the Wakefield Miracle Cycle*, which was always my favourite. At university, we had a hot debate on whether being tossed in a blanket was a light punishment for sheep-stealing, or not. Think for a minute about being thrown in a blanket by angry men, and about the lack of medical or surgical care. I come down on the side of 'not a light punishment'.

Jehan de Brie's treatise is written for *bergers et bergeres,* 'shepherds and *shep-*

AUTHOR'S NOTE

herdesses'. However practical a real shepherdess might have been, the idealization of such a life is exemplified by Queen Marie-Anoinette's game of dress-up at Le Petit Trianon. There is a tradition of pastoral literature in classical times, revived from Shakespeare's era and reaching a frenzy of rural idylls in the 18th and 19th century. Dressing up as a shepherdess, goatherd or milkmaid, frolicking with rustic men while Pan plays his pipes, is portrayed in art and literature as nostalgic and sensual, 'back to nature', with little understanding of what these jobs entail.

I wanted to show what a shepherd actually does. Medieval Christian portrayal of the shepherd lacks sentimentality while retaining that sense of a high calling, derived from the Bible. Jehan Pastor derives much of his character and daily duties from Jehan de Brie. Nici shows the medieval notion of shepherding, from a dog's point of view. I used the older word *pastou* instead of *patou* to describe the Great Pyrenees breed in the 12th century and the root of this nickname in *pastor* and *pastoral* links the work of protection dog with that of his shepherd master.

Nici brought all these skills and experiences to his life with Estela. Having been treated like a sheep by my own Great Pyrenees, I know exactly that mix of love and contempt with which they consider whether to do what you have requested of them. I also know each of them would have defended me to the death, in a heartbeat.

I have no doubt whatsoever that Nici is the ancestor of Sirius, the Great Pyrenees in *Someone To Look Up To*, who also tries to understand humans and to do his work well, but in the difficult context of modern life. I hope that reading *Nici's Tale* has taken you back to the 12th century, away from modern life, to sit on a French mountainside with a dog and a flock of sheep, eating bread and cheese with a glass of wine. These are some of my favourite things.

ABOUT THE AUTHOR

I'm a Welsh writer and photographer living in the south of France with two scruffy dogs, a beehive named 'Endeavour', a Nikon D750 and a man. I taught English in Wales for many years and my claim to fame is that I was the first woman to be a secondary headteacher in Carmarthenshire. I'm mother or stepmother to five children so life has been pretty hectic.

I've published all kinds of books, both with traditional publishers and self-published. You'll find everything under my name from prize-winning poetry and novels, military history, translated books on dog training, to a cookery book on goat cheese. My work with top dog-trainer Michel Hasbrouck has taken me deep into the world of dogs with problems, and inspired one of my novels. With Scottish parents, an English birthplace and French residence, I can usually support the winning team on most sporting occasions.

www.jeangill.com

- facebook.com/writerjeangill
- twitter.com/writerjeangill
- instagram.com/writerjeangill
- goodreads.com/JeanGill

MY BOOK RECOMMENDATIONS

If you enjoyed this book, don't miss the full story of Dragonetz and Estela's adventures, starting with

SONG AT DAWN

Book 1 in the award-winning *Troubadours Quartet.*

FREE *to members of Jean Gill's*

Special Readers' Group. Sign up at jeangill.com

'Historical Fiction at its best.' Karen Charlton, *the Detective Lavender Mysteries*

Four Discovered Diamonds Awards

Historical Novel Society Editor's Choice
Winner of the Global Ebooks Award for
Best Historical Fiction
Finalist in the Wishing Shelf Awards and
the Chaucer Awards

Set in the period following the Second Crusade, Jean Gill's spellbinding romantic thrillers evoke medieval France with breathtaking accuracy. The characters leap off the page and include amazing women like Eleanor of Aquitaine and Ermengarda of Narbonne, who shaped history in battles and in bedchambers.

CHAPTER 1

SONG AT DAWN

She woke with a throbbing headache, cramp in her legs and a curious sensation of warmth along her back. The warmth moved against her as she stretched her stiff limbs along the constraints of the ditch. She took her time before opening her eyes, heavy with too little sleep. The sun was already two hours high in the sky and she was waking to painful proof that her choice of sleeping quarters had been forced.

'I am still alive. I am here. I am no-one,' she whispered. She remembered that she had a plan but the girl who made that plan was dead. Had to be dead and stay dead. So who was she now? She needed a name.

A groan beside her attracted her attention. The strange warmth along her back, with accompanying thick white fur and the smell of damp wool, was easily identified. The girl pushed against a solid mass of giant dog, which shifted enough to let her get herself out of the ditch, where they had curved together into the sides. She recognized him well enough even though she had no idea when he had joined her in the dirt. A regular scrounger at table with the other curs, all named 'Out of my way' or worse. You couldn't mistake this one though, one of the mountain dogs bred to guard the sheep, his own coat shaggy white with brindled parts on his back and ears. Only he wouldn't stay with the flock, whatever anyone tried with him. He'd visit the fields happily enough but at the first opportunity he'd be back at the chateau. Perhaps he thought she was heading out to check on the sheep and that he'd tag along to see what he was missing.

'Useless dog,' she gave a feeble kick in his general direction. 'Can't even do one simple job. They say you're too fond of people to stay in the field with the sheep. Well, I've got news for you about people, you big stupid bastard of a useless dog. Nobody wants you.' She felt tears pricking and smeared them across her cheeks with an impatient, muddy hand. 'And if you've broken this, you'll really feel my boot.' She knelt on the edge of the ditch to retrieve an object completely hidden in a swathe of brocade.

She had counted on having the night to get away but by now there would be a search on. If Gilles had done a good job, they would find her bloody remnants well before there was any risk of them finding her living, angry self. If he had hidden the clues too well, they might keep searching until they really did find her. And if the false trail was found but too obvious, then there would be no let-up, ever. And she would never see Gilles again. She shivered, although the day was already promising the spring warmth typical of the south. She would never see Gilles again anyway, she told herself. He knew the risks as well as she did. And if it had to be done, then she was her mother's daughter and would never – 'Never!' she said aloud – forget that, whoever tried to make her. She was no longer a child but sixteen summers.

All around her, the sun was casting long shadows on the bare vineyards, buds showing on the pruned vine-stumps but no leaves yet. Like rows of wizened cats tortured on wires, the gnarled stumps bided their time. How morbid she had become these last months! Too long a winter and spent in company who considered torture-methods an amusing topic of conversation. Better to look forward. In a matter of weeks, the vines would start to green, and in another two months, the spectacular summer growth would shoot upwards and outwards but for now, all was still wintry grey.

There was no shelter in the April vineyards and the road stretched forward to Narbonne and back towards Carcassonne, pitted with the holes gouged by the severe winter of 1149. Along this road east-west, and the Via Domitia north-south, flowed the life-blood of the region, the trade and treaties, the marriage-parties and the armies, the hired escorts sent by the Viscomtesse de Narbonne and the murderers they were protection against. The girl knew all this and could list fifty fates worse than death, which were not only possible but a likely outcome of a night in a ditch. What she had forgotten was that as soon as she stood up in this open landscape, in daylight, she could see for miles – and be seen.

She looked back towards Carcassonne and chewed her lip. It was already too late. The most important reason why she should not have slept in a ditch beside the road came back to her along with the growing clatter of a large party of horse and, from the sound of it, wagons. The waking and walking was likely to be even more dangerous than the sleeping and it was upon her already.

The girl stood up straight, brushed

down her muddy skirts and clutched her brocade parcel to her breast. She knew that following her instinct to run would serve for nothing against the wild mercenaries or, at best, suspicious merchants, who were surely heading towards her. She was lucky to have passed a tranquil night – or so the night now seemed compared with the bleak prospect in front of her. What a fool to rush from one danger straight into another, forgetting the basic rules of survival on the open road. To run now would make her prey so she searched desperately for another option. In her common habit, bedraggled and dirty, she was as invisible as she could hope to be. No thief would look twice at her, nor think she had a purse to cut, far less a ransom waiting at home. No reason to bother her.

What she could not disguise was that, common or not, she was young, female and alone, and the consequences of that had been beaten into her when she was five years old and followed a cat into the forest. Not, of course, that anything bad happened in the forest, where she had lost sight of the cat but instead seen a rabbit's white scut vanishing behind a tree, as she tried to tell her father when he found her. His hard hand cut off her words, to teach her obedience for her own good, punctuated with a graphic description of the horrors she had escaped.

All that had not happened in the dappled light and crackling twigs beneath the canopy of leaves and green needles, visited her nightmares instead, with gashed faces and shuddering laughter as she ran and hid, always discovered. Until now, she *had* obeyed, and it had not been for her own good. Fool that she had been. But no more. Now she would run and hide, and not be discovered.

She drew herself up straight and tall. No, bad idea. Instead, she slumped, as ordinary as she could make herself, and felt through the slit in her dress, just below her right hip, for her other option should a quick tongue fail her. The handle fitted snugly into her hand and her fingers closed round it, reassured. The dagger was safe in its sheath, neatly attached to her under-shift with the calico ties she had laboriously sewn into the fabric in secret candle-light. She had full confidence in its blade, knowing well the meticulous care her brother gave his weapons. As to her capacity to use it, let the occasion be judge. And after that, God would be, one way or another.

By now, the oncoming chink of harness

and thud of hooves was so loud that she could hardly hear the low growl beside her. The dog was on his feet, facing the danger. He threw back his head and gave the deep bark of his kind against the wolf. The girl crossed herself and the first horse came into sight.

Dragonetz considered their progress. They had been seven days on the road since Poitiers, and many had objected to the undignified haste. Such a procession of litters, wagons and horse inevitably travelled slowly but they had kept overnight stops as simple as possible, resting at the Abbey and with loyal vassals, strengthening the ties. Apart from Toulouse of course, where Aliénor had insisted on a 'courtesy visit', her smile as polite as a dog baring its teeth. It had taken all his diplomacy to talk her out of instructing her herald to announce 'Comtesse de Toulouse' among her many titles and she had found a thousand other ways to throw her embroidered glove in the young Comte's face.

It was no easy matter to be in the service of Aliénor, Queen of France, but he would say this for her; it was never dull. The Lord be thanked that she had decided to insult Toulouse by the brevity of her stay or he could not answer for the casualties that would have ensued. Two more days of travel should see them in Narbonne and safe with Ermengarda and then he could relax his guard to the usual twenty-four hour check on every movement near Aliénor.

He was aware of the bustle behind him, wheels stopping, voices raised, and he slowed his horse almost to a standstill, anticipating the imperious voice beside him. Aliénor had tired of the litter and, mounted on her favourite palfrey, reined in beside him. He declined his head. 'My Lady.' Queen of France she might be but like all born in Aquitaine, he had sworn fealty to Aquitaine and its Duchesse, and France came second.

'Amuse me,' Aliénor instructed her companion, her pearl ear-rings spinning. The Queen's idea of dressing down for travelling might have included one less bracelet, a touch less rouge on her exquisitely painted face, and a switch of jeweled circlet, but there was little other compromise. The fur edging her dress could have been traded for a mercenary army. And that was exactly as it should be, she would have told him, had he questioned the wisdom of flaunting her status on the open road. She might have been spoiled as a child but she had been taught that a Lord of Aquitaine commanded respect as much through display and largesse as through a mailed fist, and she had learned the lesson well. In Aquitaine, she was adored. France, however, was a different country and they did things differently there.

'Once,' he began, 'there was a beautiful lady with red-gold hair, riding a white palfrey between Carcassonne and Narbonne, unaware of the danger lurking on the road ahead…'

She laughed. The pearls on her circlet gleamed and the matching ear-rings danced. Some red-gold hair escaped its net and coils under her veil. Everything about Aliénor was impatient for action. 'We have travelled more dangerous roads than this, my friend.' She was referring to their trek two years earlier, when they took the cross and the road to Damascus, the road paved with good intentions and finishing as surely in hell as anything either of them had ever known. A Crusade started in all enthusiasm and finished in shame. Each of them had good reason to bury what they had shared and he said nothing.

She rallied. 'Wouldn't you love to deal with monsters, dragons and ogres instead of Toulouse and his wet-nurses?' Her smile clouded over again. 'Or the Frankish vultures, flapping their Christian piety over me. Do you know how Paris seems to me? Black, white and grey, the northern skies, the drab clothes, the drab minds. All the colour is being leeched out of my life, month by month and I cannot continue like this.'

'You must, my Lady. It is your birthright and your birth curse. You know this.'

'I cannot exercise my birthright when I am relegated to embroidery and garden design. It is insufferable.'

'Power does not always shout its presence, my Lady, and each of the two hundred men armed behind you on this road represent a thousand more ready to die at your command. Every word you speak has the weight of those men.'

'Tell that to my husband, the Monk!' was the bitter reply. Her companion knew better than to reply to treason, especially when it came from a wife's mouth. 'Oh to be free of Sackcloth and Ashes, to hear a lute without seeing a pursed mouth or hearing that bony friar Clairvaux invoke God's punishment on the ways of Satan.'

'Clairvaux,' her companion mused, 'Bernard of Clairvaux, now what was that story about him? No, I mustn't say, not to a lady.'

'But you must, my wicked friend, that's exactly what I need, gossip. The more scurrilous the better.'

'Scurrilous gossip? About the saintly Clairvaux? How could that be possible? Anyway it's an old tale so you'll have heard it before,' he teased.

'I want to hear it again,' she ordered.

'As my Lady commands. But don't blame me if you have nightmares.'

'I already have nightmares. And Clairvaux is the least of it, curse his skinny, goose-pimpled arse.'

'You've stolen the best of my tale, my Lady, for it does indeed concern his skinny, goose-pimpled arse.'

'Tell anyway.'

'Once –'

She cut him off. 'No troubadour tricks. No romancing the rogue. He doesn't deserve it.'

'So then, even Bernard was once a young man and his body was supple, muscled, toned, bronzed and –'

'For shame!'

'You prefer I leave out some of the detail

of a young man's body? I've only just started.'

'The only toned bit of that man's body is his knees, for he is always on them, and it was ever so, whatever age he was. No, I shall have no description of him as a beautiful young man. Next part of the story, if you will.'

'I have to mention one part of the young man's anatomy, my Lady, for therein lies the story and the problem, from Bernard's point of view. He had stopped at an Inn and was served by a beautiful young serving girl, skin transparent as lace, hair golden as –'

'Yes, yes, a pretty girl. On!'

' – and poor Bernard found that part of his anatomy preferred to follow its own will rather than God's. Horrified at this inappropriate rectitude in the only situation where he would rather have been less rigid, he raced out the Inn as one possessed by a Demon, tore off his clothes and jumped into the freezing water of the village fountain, extinguishing all rebellious behaviour from his shivering, goose-pimpled body. And so ended the one and only moment when Bernard of Clairvaux wondered what a warm body would be like against his own. From then on, his body was ruled by icy regime.'

'It's not true.' Aliénor was rueful. 'He never took his clothes off.'

'My Lady, how can you doubt my word?'

'Your word as my Knight or your word as a troubadour, teller of outrageous tales?'

'The latter, my Lady,' he concurred sighing. 'But don't you think it makes a satisfying portrait – the shivering, naked monk in the fountain?'

'To the life,' she agreed. 'But I am no Bernard of Clairvaux and there are times, I too wonder what it would be like to hold a warm body against my own.' If this were an invitation, he gave no sign of taking it as such and she returned to the more entertaining subject. 'And did you hear the other one, how he ran into the street shouting that someone was trying to rob him –'

'– and it was some sinner after his virginity!'

'Must have been a blind, desperate sinner!' Aliénor called over her shoulder to the four Ladies-in-waiting keeping a discreet distance. 'Ladies, come join us. We are engaged in character destruction and the more the merrier.' As the other horses were jostled near enough to take turn-about beside the Queen, her companion's attention shifted to the road ahead, where a slight movement stabilized into an unmistakably human figure.

'Sire?' the alert came from one of his men up front.

No longer teasing, he ordered, 'My lady, you must fall back with your women. Keep to the middle. No-one sane walks this road alone and there is likely a trap ahead.' He had already moved ahead, throwing orders behind him as he caught up with his hand-picked vanguard. He glanced over his shoulder, satisfied that Aliénor was already invisible in the middle of a thick shield of armoured men.

Swords out, reins tight in one hand, they advanced on the lone figure standing at the roadside, who seemed to get smaller as they grew nearer.

'It's a woman, Sire!' his man exclaimed.

'Be on guard, Danton, a woman can have a band of cut-throats on hand as easily as a man,' but there was as much chance of hiding men in the open vineyards around them as behind a molehill. He sheathed his sword, and a signal passed back along the line in a wave of relief.

The Commander reined in beside a girl who stood stock-still, a great hound at her side, growling menaces. The entire procession ground to a halt behind its leader and

Danton jumped out the saddle, sword unsheathed, eyes on the dog.

'No!' came instinctively from the girl, who stepped forward, interposing a reckless arm between Danton's approaching sword and the growling dog. Her other arm clutched some sort of large bundle close to her chest.

'No,' agreed the Commander, looking fixedly at the girl. 'Danton, I think the puppy would benefit from some space while we decide whether to slit its throat or not.' Danton backed off but kept his sword ready. It was obvious to all there that his leader was not only referring to the dog. 'You see,' he said gently, 'we can't be sure that you won't run across the fields, then get ahead of us and prepare your bandit-friends to slit our throats and steal our valuables. And that just wouldn't do.'

The girl looked at him, astonished. 'But I'm on my own!' Topaz eyes, like those of the hunting leopards in Alexandria, green shadows and muddy depths, sparks where there should have been fear. Topaz eyes and black hair, silky as the tents of the Moorish armies. Olive skin like a slave girl but smooth, unpitted, ripe. Her clothes spoke of the servant but the fire in her eyes did not.

Even more gently, he told her, 'We just

can't take the risk. And so that gives us two choices.' She didn't move but he could see the movement of her long throat as she swallowed. 'Either Danton here is allowed to exercise his duty and his sword —' She neither flinched nor spoke. Interesting. Physical courage combined with the good sense not to provoke him. ' — or we must invite you to join our company.' Was that a frown? There was definitely some mystery here.

'What *is* going on?' Aliénor pushed her horse through to stand shoulder to shoulder beside the Commander's. 'Can't we just get on with the journey?'

'We can, my Lady, as soon as you tell me whether I must have this maid run through or packed with the other baggage.'

For a heartbeat he thought he had misjudged his Queen and that finally her wildness had overcome her humanity. Aliénor studied the girl. Then, after a tortuous pause that stabbed a hundred times, 'She has something to hide,' Aliénor stated, in a tone that reminded everyone present why they followed her. 'Muddy servant's clothes, alone by a ditch on the busiest road in Occitania… Who are you and what are you doing here?'

The girl looked down but she said nothing.

'No! Don't hit her,' the Commander and Aliénor spoke as one to prevent Danton showing what he thought of dumb insolence to the Queen. 'If you are told to hit her, you must deal with the dog first, not second, I think you'll find,' the Commander added unnecessarily, as the dog snapped the air where Danton had nearly been.

'Quite,' said Aliénor, her gaze level and merciless on the girl. 'As you see, it is dangerous to ignore me, and suggests guilt. What is in that package?'

'My belongings,' the girl muttered.

'Well, that wasn't so hard to say, was it,' Aliénor's eyes narrowed. 'Now open it up,' she ordered. The girl hesitated and Aliénor's voice steeled further. 'Either you open it yourself or Danton kills the dog, which he is very keen to do, and then it is opened by force while you are held very, very roughly by the arms. And then it gets worse, much worse. Am I clear?'

The girl's answer was to lay the brocade down on the rough stone. As she bent down, her hair swung clear of her neck and the Commander revised his first impression. Her skin was not flawless; a badly healed scar marred the clear skin of her left shoulder. His professional eye judged it to be deliberate, and whip rather than blade. With tenderness, she unwrapped her precious object until it was laid bare on the outspread brocade.

The musical instrument revealed was of reddish wood, so highly polished that the girl's figure gleamed dully in the deep, pear-shaped bowl. Three circles of cream enamel inlay decorated the wood, each with a design of arabesques and interlaced points. Eight strings, frets, a bent peg-board for tuning.

'Al-Oud,' he breathed.

She looked puzzled. 'It's a mandora.'

'And obviously stolen.' One of Aliénor's Ladies had edged forward. At first sight, she was no less magnificent than her mistress, but whereas Aliénor's finery was merely the setting for Aliénor herself, this Lady was diminished by her trappings. Her painted face seemed set as a mask, her fur trimming too broad as if to compensate for lesser quality, her jeweled ear-rings too glittery, obviously paste to a connoisseur. 'Cut off her hand and let's be done with her.'

'And your reasoning in this?' Aliénor asked quietly. No-one doubted her willingness to judge and, if that be the judgement, sentence as proposed. No-one questioned that the girl's hand was forfeit for her theft. Most would have judged this lenient, for such an instrument was a unique treasure. Had they not been on the road, the girl could be an example to others, could be caged, and tormented by the public before the next phase of a long, slow death. No-one present would have flinched at such a necessity, although some would have enjoyed it more than others. However, they were on the road and there was no time for such deliberation.

'My Lady, how would a servant come by such a thing, except dishonestly – and servant she clearly is, by her clothes. And I can think of only one thing a woman might be doing alone on this road! My guess is that she has stolen this instrument and fled, offering her legs in the air, until she can sell her other goods at market. She couldn't even tell you her name, my Lady! What more proof of guilt do you need!'

The girl's eyes blazed but she just picked up the mandora and clutched it to her. Aliénor's eyes met those of her Commander as the fingers of the girl's left hand found their habitual place on the frets and she cradled the instrument in the position they had seen a thousand times, in every banquet hall of the civilized world.

'The proof is easy,' Aliénor declared. 'If the instrument is yours, play for us, girl.'

Amid the jangles and snorts of restless horses, the mutterings of people impatient to get on, and the birdsong of amorous April, the girl closed her eyes. She thrummed the strings, adjusted the pegs and cleared her throat. Then she sang a scale. The sweetness of the simple ut re mi fa so la already held promise and when she opened her eyes and wound her voice round the strings in perfect harmony, the company around her hushed. The well-known words of the Aubade, the Dawn Song, floated like apple blossom on the breeze and the dog lay down, silent, beside the singer.

> *'A-bed beside his lady-love,*
> *Her own true knight stopped kissing.*
> *'My sweet, my own, what shall we do?*
> *Day is nigh and night is over*
> *We must be parted, my self missing*
> *All the day away from you.'*

> *If only day would never come*
> *If only night could spare the pain*
> *Of each new parting, little Death*
> *That leaves enough to die again.*

*The Watchman calls the hour of
   Dawning
Bids me stand and face the day,
Exiles me to constant Morning
Grieving that I must away.*

*Know that whereso'er I wander
Never shall I find true rest
Without the circle of your kisses
And may you love your Night the best.*

*'My sweet, my own, what shall we do?
Day is nigh and night is over
We must be parted, my self missing
All the day away from you.'*

The last notes of the mandora hung plaintive in the air as Danton sheathed his sword.

'You have answered the charge of theft and we find you innocent,' Aliénor's measured voice broke the spell. 'What have you to say, that you refuse to give your name to me?'

'I do have a name to give you, my Lady. My songster's name is Estela de Matin.'

'Then Estela de Matin it shall be and such a musician is always welcome at my court, whether man or woman. If you would like to join us, we can explore the mysteries surrounding you at our leisure.'

If the girl saw the mailed fist in the glove of this 'invitation' she gave no sign but curtsied acceptance and wrapped up her instrument again in its brocade.

'What do you think?' Aliénor asked her Commander.

'A sweet voice but empty,' was the verdict. 'It lacks the maturity the song needs.'

'What made you choose that one, of all the songs?' Aliénor asked the girl, who had looked down, hiding her flushed face, but now raised her eyes to meet the Commander's.

'I love the song,' she said simply. 'It is the work of a Master and it seemed right to me and I thought everyone would know the song…' she tailed off.

'You chose well,' Aliénor told her. 'And yes, we know the song, don't we.'

'Too well, my Lady.' The Commander excused himself and rode back down the line.

A bulky man, with wild black hair and beard, pushed his horse to the front. 'My Lady, I am sent for the girl.'

'Take her, Raoulf and see that she is comfortable.' Raoulf dismounted, took a step toward Estela and the dog half-rose. 'No, dog,' she told him. 'Go! You are not my dog! I don't want you. Go away!' The dog watched but made no move as she went towards Raoulf. He lifted her onto his saddle, with her mandora, as easily as if she were a puppet, then he jumped up behind her. A dainty boot lashed out at Estela's shins as she passed, with a murmured 'So sorry,' that dripped poison and smelled strongly of musk. Estela would remember the smell but for now she was beyond caring. There was just one question to resolve before she gave in to an overwhelming weariness, of body and spirit.

'Who is your Commander?' she asked Raoulf.

'You're not going to pretend you don't know,' was the strange reply.

'Truly,' she pressed.

'Dragonetz los Pros, of course,' he stated, as if it was obvious. And it should have been.

'I thought he would be older,' she said. Dragonetz, Aliénor's knight, who had earned his title 'los Pros', 'the Brave', as a Crusader, when so many had come home with titles like 'Brown-britches.' Dragonetz, the Master Troubadour, the writer of the song she had presumed to sing in front of him. And the inanities she had come out with! He would think it deliberate! Her cheeks burned and she was only too pleased to be unloaded like a sack of corn onto a simple mattress in a wagon. When Raoulf pulled a coverlet over her with his calloused hands, and told her to rest now, she responded automatically, 'Thank you, Gilles,' and drifted with the bump bump rhythm of the wagon into deepest sleep.

If you loved Nici and want to read about one of his descendants, try

Someone to Look Up To.

Top Pick Award from Litpick Student Reviews. By IPPY and Global Ebook Award Winning author. For all dog-lovers!

'Jean Gill has captured the innermost thoughts of this magnificent animal.' Les Ingham, Pyr International

A dog's life in the south of France. From puppyhood, Sirius the Pyrenean Mountain Dog has been trying to understand his humans and train them with kindness.

How this led to their divorce he has no idea. More misunderstandings take Sirius to

Death Row in an animal shelter, as a so-called dangerous dog learning survival tricks from the other inmates. During the twilight barking, he is shocked to hear his brother's voice but the bitter-sweet reunion is short-lived. Doggedly, Sirius keeps the faith.

One day, his human will come.

Jean Gill's Publications

Novels
Someone to Look Up To: a dog's search for love and understanding *(The 13th Sign)* 2016

Natural Forces
Book 2 Arrows Tipped with Honey *(The 13th Sign)* 2020
Book 1 Queen of the Warrior Bees *(The 13th Sign)* 2019

The Troubadours Quartet
Book 5 Nici's Christmas Tale: A Troubadours Short Story *(The 13th Sign)* 2018
Book 4 Song Hereafter *(The 13th Sign)* 2017
Book 3 Plaint for Provence *(The 13th Sign)* 2015
Book 2 Bladesong *(The 13th Sign)* 2015
Book 1 Song at Dawn *(The 13th Sign)* 2015

Love Heals
Book 2 More Than One Kind *(The 13th Sign)* 2016
Book 1 No Bed of Roses *(The 13th Sign)* 2016

Looking for Normal (teen fiction/fact)
Book 1 Left Out *(The 13th Sign)* 2017
Book 2 Fortune Kookie *(The 13th Sign)* 2017

Non-fiction/Memoir/Travel
How Blue is my Valley *(The 13th Sign)* 2016
A Small Cheese in Provence *(The 13th Sign)* 2016
Faithful through Hard Times *(The 13th Sign)* 2018
4.5 Years – war memoir by David Taylor *(The 13th Sign)* 2017

Short Stories and Poetry
One Sixth of a Gill *(The 13th Sign)* 2014
From Bedtime On *(The 13th Sign)* 2018 (2nd edition)
With Double Blade *(The 13th Sign)* 2018 (2nd edition)

Translation (from French)
The Last Love of Edith Piaf – Christie Laume *(Archipel)* 2014
A Pup in Your Life – Michel Hasbrouck 2008
Gentle Dog Training – Michel Hasbrouck *(Souvenir Press)* 2008

www.ingramcontent.com/pod-product-compliance
Ingram Content Group UK Ltd.
Pitfield, Milton Keynes, MK11 3LW, UK
UKHW042000230426
12048UKWH00009B/436